i

Floating Cloud

A Taelo Story: Floating Cloud

By: *Ron Mueller*

Around the World Publishing, LLC
4914 Cooper Road Suite 144
Cincinnati, Ohio 45242-9998

This story is a work of fiction. Names, characters, places, and incidents either are products of the author's imagination or are used fictitiously. Any resemblance to actual events or locales or persons, living or dead, is entirely coincidental.

ISBN 13: 978-1-68223-207-1
ISBN 10: 1-68223-207-7

Distributed by Ingram
Cover Design By: Ron Mueller
Cover Picture By: Hien Mueller

ଛ Dedicated to: All fit grandmothers who have raised their children's children.

Floating Cloud

Floating Cloud sat on the lakeside path with her dead daughter on her lap. Silent Pool's last words were "I am with Fast Skimmer. Please take good care of Quiet Rabbit." Then she closed her eyes and with a smile on her lips she let out a long breath and was gone. Floating Cloud knew that her will to live had left her moons ago when she lost her soul mate.

Floating Cloud looked up into the clear blue sky. Her tears ran freely down her cheeks. She had watched Silent Pool look up and smile, then trip over a limp, fall backward and hit her head on a stone. It was as if she had seen where she was going. Her smile was the first since Fast Skimmer had been killed.

Floating Cloud thought back at her own similar experience. Her parents had not approved of the person she had chosen as her mate. Her mother had sent her on her way declaring that her family name was now Black Cloud. She and her mate had made their own way for almost twenty moon cycles then they came upon the Elk Hide Clan and had been accepted.

It was an overwhelming shock when, that fall season, she lost her mate during the first hunt. He fell from a cliff as he tried to run down a small boar.

She had been devastated but her love for Silent Pool had sustained her.

Silent Pool was the reason she had recovered. She was born on a spring morning like the one she had now died on. Floating Cloud thought back to all the times her daughter had saved her from the darkness that often threatened to consume her. She knew that she had not been able to give that relief back to Silent Pool.

Now she sat and cried.

She stood and picked up Silent Pool and slowly carried her back to the Elk Campsite. She would take her to the Shaman of the Next Life who would prepare her for the journey to the land of the Ancestors.

White Swan came to her and helped carry Silent Pool. She asked what had happened. She listened as Floating Cloud described what had taken place and her interpretation of it.

White Swan commented on how sad she was. Fast Skimmer had been a good friend and when he and Silent Pool became mates, she too became a good friend.

She shared the fact that it had been clear to everyone how much Silent Pool missed her mate.

White Swan left Floating Cloud with the Shaman but told her to come to her camp site when she was through. She would have Quiet Rabbit there.

Silent Pool had once again given Floating Cloud a reason to stay young. She would need all her strength to care for and raise her grand-daughter Quiet Rabbit. She would need Quiet Rabbit as much as Quiet Rabbit would need her.

When she saw White Swan approaching, Quiet Rabbit knew that something was wrong. When she was invited to have the morning meal at White Swan's campsite, she knew it was bad. She was trembling as she walked with White Swan to her camp.

Taelo was sitting on a log near the fire. He looked at her and pointed to a seat near to him. He pointed to a leather sack hanging near the fire and said that the morning stew would make them all feel better.

Quiet Rabbit looked at Grey Fox Running. He seemed to have the same tears in his eyes that he had on the day he brought her father home. She immediately had tears in her eyes. She knew instantly that Floating Cloud would come to tell her that her mother was gone. She began to silently cry.

She felt Taelo's arm go around her shoulder. He gave her a hug and quietly told her his heart hurt too. He told her to look at the clouds in the sky and imaging floating there with her father and mother.

Floating Cloud took in the scene around White Swan's cook fire. She paused for a moment, took a deep breath before going on.

She tried to keep her composure as she approached Quiet Rabbit. She was not sure how she was going to break the news.

Quiet Rabbit looked up at Floating Cloud and saw tears in her eyes. It was clear to her that everyone was crying. It was also obvious that her mother was not there. She knew in her heart that her mother was with her father. It was where her mother wished to be. A shiver ran through her. She closed her eyes and wished her mother happiness.

She looked up at her grandmother and patted the seat next to herself as Taelo had done for her.

She looked around and quietly said what everyone seemed to be avoiding, "My mother is with father. It is as she wished. Later I will want to hear how she made the journey. Now I think it is time we all enjoyed the morning stew."

Floating Cloud was surprised by Quiet Rabbit's immediate understanding and how she handled the situation. She was acting more mature than her twelve seasons' age. She also knew that it would take time for her to really come to terms with the loss of her mother.

She sat down and asked whether the stew was ready. She once again thanked her own mate for having made good friends with Grey Fox Running, White Swan, Quiet Pheasant, White Swan's sister, and Red Oak. She knew they would support her and Quiet Rabbit.

Departing two sun cycles later to go to the clan meeting was a change that both Floating Cloud and Quiet Rabbit needed.

Floating Cloud packed all the things that had been made and prepared for trading. This preparation was more emotional than Floating Clout had anticipated.

Silent Pool had worked hard to prepare for this event. She had many items to trade. She had planned to make this trip and had planned for success.

It was clear to Floating Cloud that her death on the path was an accident. Silent pool had planned to make sure she could raise her daughter just as she had done.

Floating Cloud made a vow to get the best deals possible. It was going to be harder in the future for Quiet Rabbit and her to have this much to trade. They would be on their own and it would be hard for them to accumulate the materials and have the time to make goods to trade.

Little did she know the granddaughter she would raise would be a leader among all the clans.

The journey to the Elk Clan's meeting valley was bordered on each side by mountains and had the effect of allowing the events of the past several moon cycles to dissipate in intensity. The ache would be long. But its leaving would happen, and it would remain at a manageable level.

As they traveled, every morning, Floating Cloud would find a rabbit, ground hog or several squirrels lying outside her enclosure.

She was not sure who the generous person might be, but she had her suspicions. She was pleased that someone was concerned enough to make sure that she and Quiet Rabbit had a good morning meal and that there would be enough for a second meal.

A few sun cycles later she stood with the rest of the clan looking down at the small oblong lake and the valley where all the Elk Clan was gathered for the Elk Clan meeting. The Elk Hide Clan was the last to arrive.

Floating Cloud listened as Taelo suggested that the Elk Hide Clan make their camp on the far side of the lake. Their clan would be the first to camp on the far side. The only thing preventing this had been the need to cross the small river that fed the lake. He proposed putting up a way to walk across.

She was pleased when Wise Owl assigned Taelo the task of leading a team to build a bridge across the stream that fed the lake. He was to signal success to the clan by lighting a fire and sending up white smoke.

When the sun reached the zenith and the white smoke signal rose up into the air, she raised her voice and shouted enthusiastically with the rest of the clan. She knew it would be a good meeting and that she and Quite Rabbit would not be carrying water very far.

She took Quite Rabbit's hand and they marched past all the other sub-clans on their way to a lakeside camp.

She made sure they both were displaying their best trade garments as they walked proudly to their premier campsite.

In the sun cycles that followed, her aggressive trading paid off. She traded for several gorgeous outfits and additional footwear. Each sun cycle she made a visit to the one camp that specialized in snacks and treats. There she would get some small treat for both herself and for Quiet Rabbit.

She was spoiling them both and enjoying it.

The meeting progressed smoothly. Then she learned that Grey Fox Running would be leaving the Elk Hide Clan to become the leader of the original Elk Clan.

Floating Cloud went to White Swan to confirm the rumor she had heard. When White Swan confirmed the change of sub-clan, Floating Cloud immediately asked if she and Quiet Rabbit could join the Elk Clan.

She knew that this change would be good for her as well as for Quiet Rabbit. It would be a fresh start for them both.

She returned to Quiet Rabbit to tell her about the change.

She was again surprised by Quiet Rabbit.

Quiet Rabbit had overheard Taelo and Golden Hawk talking about their move to the Elk Clan.

She immediately wanted to do the same. She did not wish to return to the place where she had lost both her mother and father.

When Floating Cloud approached, the look on her face shouted out that she too wanted to join the Elk Clan.

When Floating Cloud asked whether Quiet Rabbit was interested in joining the Elk Clan, Quiet Rabbit smiled and gave her grandmother a hug and whispered a thank you and a yes.

Once the change of leaders for the Elk Clan was announced, and Grey Fox Running accepted her, Floating Cloud, let Wise Owl know about her desire to change clans.

She felt relieved when Wise Owl agreed with her that it was a good move and would provide a way for both she and Quiet Rabbit to find new happiness.

Her next shock came when all the other clans had left the valley. Grey Fox Running and Red Oak asked that all the Elk Clan families display their food supply. Except for Grey Fox Running and Red Oak, she had almost as much for her and Quiet Rabbit than all the food the other families possessed.

She realized the Elk Clan was in dire a straight and realized why Silent Hawk, the leader that had brought the Elk Clan to the meeting willingly accepted Grey Fox Running as the immediate leader for the Elk Clan and Red Oak as a lead hunter.

The Elk Clan has lost their lead hunter to a rhino attack. The hunt had gone very badly. The Elk Clan was on the verge of running out of food. They would not last until the winter solstice unless the ancients acted.

She was somewhat alarmed when two-thirds of her food was redistributed to the various clan families. This meant that even by rationing and cutting back she would be out of food by the solstice.

She kept quiet she trusted that Grey Fox Running and Red Oak would successfully guide the Elk Clan, but she worried. She did not have a hunter to resupply her.

Floating Cloud was surprised that the rabbits and other small game kept appearing at her cook fire. This was a great comfort to her.

When each morning the food for the day was at her cooking ring, it was clear that the person she suspected was now with her in the Elk Clan. This gave her new hope.

When Taelo came in with the news that he and Golden Hawk had found a large hive of honeybees Floating Cloud gave a sigh of relief.

Taelo and Golden Hawk seemed to be single handedly giving the Elk Clan reason to believe that they would survive the cold weather that had engulfed them. The honey was abundant, and all the families received a share.

The elk and deer left on the trail by Brave Deer's hunting party was the next event that signaled to the clan that they would most likely survive the winter.

Floating Cloud tried to catch her benefactor in the act of leaving the rabbits and other small game at her campfire, but it was clear that she was not going to catch that person in the act.

Not many sun cycles later, as they passed a valley branching off to the side of the direction of the clan's travel, an eagle's cry came from the air.

White Swan insisted that the Elk Clan stop and make camp early. She insisted Taelo and Golden Hawk, who had left the clan to scout the surrounding area, were facing some trial and they might need help.

Floating Cloud vocally supported White Swan. Quiet Pheasant was also insistent. It was clear to Silent Hawk, who in Grey Fox Running's absence was temporarily leading the clan, that he would have little choice. He did the wise thing and called for an early halt.

When late in the night, Taelo and Golden Hawk returned, Floating Cloud and Quiet Rabbit were among the first to help them pull the travois carrying a large elk and two enormous dire wolf skins.

The wolf skins were so large that at first the old hunters thought the hides might be bear hides. Two wolves of the size of the hides would have easily defeated two skilled hunters. They wondered how two hunters as young and inexperienced as Taelo and Golden Hawk could possibly have killed them.

Floating Cloud offered to treat the hides and make a coat and vest for Taelo and Golden Hawk.

White Swan thanked her and accepted the offer. She jokingly asked what Floating Cloud would do with the second hide.

The next morning instead of rabbit or some other small game, her suspicion was confirmed when she instead found a large block of elk meat by her cook fire.

She never had any doubt about who had been leaving her the food but now she wondered how he was able to do so and never be seen.

A few sun cycles later the clan arrived at the seaside.

It was clear to her by Taelo and Golden Hawk's frozen leggings that they had been to the sea ahead of the clan.

She offered both of them a dry set of newly made dire wolf skin clothing. Taelo smiled and thanked her for being so kind and took her up on the offer.

White Swan watched as Taelo accepted the dire wolf long pants. She too had noticed the frozen pants both he and Golden Hawk were in.

She walked over to Taelo and complimented him on the dire wolf outfit just as he was putting on the matching jacket. She felt the soft inner lining of the jacket and looked over at Floating Cloud with her eyebrows raised. She whispered what a jacket and thanked her for doing such excellent work and doing it so quickly.

Silent Hawk surprised the Elk Clan members by asking White Swan to scout down the coast for a suitable winter camp for the clan. He would go up the coast and do the same.

If a suitable location was found the clan was to follow the first team that returned and begin to immediately set up the camp.

Floating Cloud was not surprised when White Swan quickly accepted and asked Quiet Pheasant to be her partner. Nor was she surprised when Taelo and Golden Hawk both said they were also going.

She took note that the two had not asked but declared their participation. The two were already demonstrating the leadership that she had recognized in them.

She was surprised when she volunteered but was rejected. White Swan thanked her but told her to get everyone ready to follow her when she returned.

Two sun cycles later Floating Cloud watched as the four returned. White Swan and Quiet Pheasant were moving at a good jogging pace, but it was clear that Taelo and Golden Hawk were having no problem keeping that pace.

She was sure the two younger members could easily out pace their mothers.

Floating Cloud listened as various Elk Clan members resisted following White Swan to the location she had found.

She picked up her belongings and loudly declared she was ready to follow White Swan. She watched as one of the shy young Elk Clan young women followed her lead.

White Swan turned, ordered the Clan to follow and went down the beach. She never looked back.

Floating Cloud and Quiet Rabbit kept up a tally of the number that were following. Finally, they announced that every person on the beach was following.

White Swan and Quiet Pheasant fell back and thanked each person for following them. Floating Cloud listened as they gave a work assignment to each person. The two had already picked the location for the large clan lodge and had determined that the digging and material collection would begin when they arrived at the site.

When they arrived at the location, Floating Cloud immediately fell in love with it.

There was a spit, made up of a tall craggily cliff curving out to sea. It had a monstrous round boulder opposite the cliff that created a quiet inner cove. There was a flat beach area where the entire clan could set up their camp ran back to a cliff.

She immediately staked out her choice for her campsite near a small, sweet water stream that made its way across the beach to the foot of spit cliffs.

She concluded that it would be the best camp that she had experienced in her lifetime.

White Swan's immediate push to erect a central clan lodge enrolled every able-bodied person.

Quiet Rabbit commented that she had never worked so hard. Floating Cloud gave her a hug and asked if they had made the right choice?

Quiet Rabbit replied that she would not want it any other way.

Silver Hawk returned as the main lodge took its final shape. Every hide had been used to create a warm enclosure but the homes for individual families would have to wait until the three long hunter teams returned.

Floating Cloud listened as Silver Hawk praised White Swan's leadership and the clan members for the hard work. It was clear to her that White Swan had been raised to a new level of respect.

Floating Cloud had copied the in-ground design used for the lodge to build her hutch. She and Quiet Rabbit had dug out and built a snug hutch that provided them enough room for each to have their sleeping area on opposite sides and a back area to store their personal goods. They had made the walls of stone and had put the main cross member poles across the tops of the stone wall that was about half their height above the ground. Since they had no large animal hides, they had woven small willow branches into a mat and had covered the mat with grass.

The two had given each other a hug when they put the last bundle of grass into place. They both commented that it would keep out the snow and the cold but wondered if in the spring it would keep out the rain.

A small fire at the entrance kept the interior warm.

They shared their design with the rest of the clan, but a hard snow presented a barrier for the other families to dig and build something similar. Floating Cloud knew that they had been lucky to get their hutch done.

She was relieved when Brave Deer and his hunting group returned. But the physical condition of the hunters was a shock. Their tale of being attacked by a pack of dire wolves put new fear in her heart about the forest and animals around them. She was reminded of Taelo's and Golden Hawk's encounter with dire wolves that she now figured had attacked Brave Deer and his hunters. She again thought about the two and realized that they had on their own passed the test of being hunters and warriors.

She was glad to be on the isolated beach front that was protected on three sides. Her enthusiasm for building a wall from the beach back to the cliff, as suggested by White Swan, went up dramatically. It seemed to her that everyone else had the same reaction.

A moon cycle later Red Oak and his hunters returned with four heavily load travois of meat. Floating Cloud and Quiet Rabbit listened as he told of the attack of a band of Others.

Floating Cloud was disturbed by this tale.

She listened as White Swan and Quiet Pheasant discussed their plan to address the presence of a Clan of Others up the coast. She agreed with them that an approach showing concern and kindness would work better than a show of force. She had heard that the Others were very ferocious fighters.

Once again, she was turned down when she volunteered to go along with White Swan. She understood the rejection but she none the less wanted to show her support in a direct way.

When resistance was voiced by some clan members, she openly and publicly praised White Swan for such a level-headed approach.

She and Quiet Rabbit were on the beach and watched as White Swan, Quiet Pheasant, Golden Hawk and Taelo left with their food and gift loaded travois.

Silver Hawk had yielded to White Swan. He stood next to Floating Cloud and commented that the women of the clan were clearly as brave as any of the hunters and warriors.

It was only three sun cycles later as she and Quiet Rabbit sat on their favorite beach side boulder that they saw White Swan and Quiet Pheasant jogging toward them. They were by themselves.

Floating Cloud's initial concern about the absence of Taelo and Golden Hawk dissipated when she watched the relaxed way White Swan and Quiet Pheasant were moving and conversing.

She turned to Quiet Rabbit and commented that they would ask about Taelo and Golden Hawk but that it was clear there was no trouble.

White Swan's tale of her meeting with the Clan of Others and Taelo knocking out a huge young man had the Elk Clan members spell bound. The fact that the Others had been waiting for Taelo was a surprise.

Floating Cloud remembered the Naming Day when Taelo had selected the claw of an eagle and the eagle that had been circling for the entire time made a steep dive and plucked the claw from his up stretched hand.

It turned out that event had somehow become part of the Clan of Others heritage. He had been expected but the fact that he was a members of the New Ones had surprised the Others.

She and Quiet Rabbit made good use of the large elk hide given them by Red Oak before his departure to get Grey Fox Running. They oiled it and stretched it over their woven mat of branches that made up the roof of their hutch.

They immediately experienced a new warm interior. They were now certain that the spring rains would be kept out.

It was only a few sun cycles later when after the sun had dipped below the far horizon. She and Quiet Rabbit were still sitting on their favorite shore side boulder when White Swan let out the eagle cry that she used to identify herself to her family.

Two replies came back.

Grey Fox Running and his hunters were approaching with several travois of meat. The surprise was that Taelo, and Golden Hawk had returned at the same time.

The bigger surprise was that they were escorted by four warriors of the Others.

Floating Cloud hugged Quiet Rabbit as they watched Grey Fox Running greet the Others and invite them into the Elk Clans Home.

She learned that the huge Other warrior, whose name was Burley Bear, was the person Taelo had knocked out. That event had bonded Burley Bear to Taelo.

Winter hit hard.

The weather became a challenge and the cold crept in along the floor and chilled one's feet. She and Quiet Rabbit huddled by their warming fire.

They had moved it to the center of their hutch and made an opening in the roof above it. Even so they each wore a rabbit skin vest and had on rabbit skin lined knee-high boots.

They learned of Taelo's and Golden Hawk's departure on the morning that they watched Burley Bear climb the cliff as he went out to find them.

Floating Cloud wondered out loud why the two would pick the heart of a cold winter to do such a thing.

Quiet Rabbit replied that they were probably responding to a call from the Ancients.

Floating Cloud worried as the weather became worse and the cold became threatening. She worried about where Taelo and Golden Hawk might find shelter.

Her other concern was about the clan's food supply. She had listened to Grey Fox Running comment on the potential need to send out a group of hunters when the weather improved.

She made sure the two of them had one good meal every morning. She kept a hot stew by the fire for the afternoon meal. They were both losing weight. Everyone in camp was having the same problem.

Several moon cycles later, when she and Quiet rabbit could count the few number of sun cycles of food they had left, a scout came and let Grey Fox Running know that strangers were coming toward them along the beach from the south.

Quiet Rabbit grabbed her hand and together they followed Grey Fox Running to the top of the spit cliffs.

On the way to the top of the cliff she heard Quiet Rabbit comment that she was sure it was Taelo returning.

Floating Cloud had no idea how Quiet Rabbit would have known that it was Taelo, but she was right.

The entire Elk Clan celebrated the return of all three young hunters who had pulled back a sled loaded with three young buffalo. Even better they had brought the news that the buffalo herd spent their winter in what the three had named the Valley of Plenty.

The Elk Clan now had ample food and therefore of hides.

Spring brought out the small blue and yellow flowers on the side of the spit's cliffs. Their campsite was warmed by the sun and Floating Cloud experienced new energy. The sea, the cliffs and the warm sun gave the entire clan a feeling of well-being.

When Taelo and Golden Hawk began building their fish trap she enthusiastically supported Quiet Rabbit and her two new friends Busy Bee and Talking Wren as they organized the younger clan members to help build the trap.

She was not surprised at the success of the fish trap and the fact that it engaged the entire Elk Clan as the fish were caught, processed, and dried. She had been present when a much younger Taelo had changed how the Elk Hide Clan had captured their spring salmon with a much smaller version of the trap.

She was astounded when Taelo, Golden Hawk and Burley Bear killed a giant shark that had entered the fish trap. It was so large that the shark was processed like it was a buffalo.

She and a group of volunteers stretched the shark skin for processing. She let White Swan know that she would use the shark skin as White Swan desired.

She reinforced Taelo's public recognition of Quiet Rabbit, Busy Bee, and Talking Wren for their contribution in building the fish trap. He had given them the best and most teeth, but he had shared the teeth with all the clan members.

Floating Cloud commented to Quiet Rabbit that the generosity shown by the Taelo, Golden Hawk and Burley Bear spoke of their high character.

Quiet Rabbit smiled and put her hand to her heart but said nothing.

The fishing was so successful that it was reduced to only a few hours a day.

A flat stone area along the spit was turned into a salt making area. She and Quiet Rabbit claimed a square that was two spear lengths long. Each day they would carefully scrape off the dried white sea salt and then put more salt water on their square. The sun then did the job of evaporating the water and making a new layer of salt.

Floating Cloud was relieved by the fact that she and Quiet Rabbit were not going to be destitute.

They would have a very large supply of salt. They had a very large supply of dried fish. They ate fresh fish or meat each day.

And Quiet Rabbit and her two friends had become the supplier of small game and a variety of roots and berries.

Floating Cloud commented on their success and complemented Quiet Rabbit for her ability to supply so much food.

The spit was the home of thousands of seagulls and other birds. She and Quiet Rabbit gathered many eggs for their meals.

The spit was also covered in blueberries. The two of them gathered berries to eat fresh but they also cooked them and made a jam that could be kept for future use and to trade.

Floating Cloud felt a warmth flow through her when White Swan suggested that Quiet Rabbit should volunteer to go on a long hunt with Taelo and Golden Hawk.

She asked if any other young women would go as well.

White Swan let her know that she was making the same suggestion to Busy Bee and Talking Wren. These were Quiet Rabbits best friends.

Floating Cloud knew the answer to her question to Quiet Rabbit by the look of pleasure she saw.

She gave Quiet Rabbit a hug and told her that it would be an adventure of a lifetime.

Not long after the hunt began, she watched as Little Beaver and Talking Wren returned with a young bull pulling a travois loaded with a huge supply of meat.

The novelty of an animal pulling a travois and the amount of meat that the team had sent back impressed the entire Clan.

The story of the first hunt and how both Taelo, hunting with Quiet Rabbit, Golden Hawk, hunting with Busy Bee had each killed four buffalo in one hunt, had Floating Cloud feeling like her name. She knew that Quiet Rabbit had wanted to hunt with Taelo. She knew Quiet Rabbit's intent and approved.

She noticed that both White Swan and Quiet Pheasant had smiles as they looked at each other.

Floating Cloud complemented Little Otter and Talking Wren and sent a sack full of honey for the team to enjoy.

Floating Cloud publicly made the point that the team, the leaders had predicted would do poorly, had outperformed the other hunt teams many times over.

She was not going to let the leaders forget their negative view of the women of the clan being hunting partners.

The return of the hunters led by Little Otter and the four meat loaded travois that by themselves was more than the other three long hunt teams had brought in sealed Floating Cloud's assessment of Taelo's and Golden Hawk's hunting skill.

Floating Cloud also took in who was walking with whom. Quiet Rabbit was at Taelo's side, Busy Bee was at Golden Hawk's side and Talking Wren was talking to Little Otter.

She knew that Quite Pool, looking down from the land of the Ancients would be pleased.

A few sun cycles later she was sitting with White Swan and Quiet Pheasant. The sun was on its way to kiss the sea at its horizon.

Taelo, Quiet Rabbit, Golden Hawk and Busy Bee were walking along the beach and talking to each other.

Both White Swan and Quiet Pheasant wistfully commented on the scene and the fact that their sons seemed have decided on their mates.

Floating Cloud smiled and commented that it was reassuring when soulmate met soulmate and wasn't this what the two of them had wanted.

The End

Thank you for reading to this point!

The Stories of Taelo are set in the distant past, long before the time currently given as to when people migrated into the western hemisphere.

This is purposely done since the stories are meant to engage the reader in a story and not relate exact history.

The adventures of Taelo and Golden Hawk provide the backdrop for stories featuring the values of treating others as you wish to be treated, of responsibility, integrity, honesty and of contribution, and the joy of learning.

About the Author

Ronald E. Mueller
remwriter95@gmail.com

Ron grew up in what is now Flint River State Park in Southeast Iowa. The 170-year-old house Ron lived in is built into a hillside. It faces a 125-foot-high cliff towering over the little Flint River. The house and the land talked to him about; the passing of time, the struggle to conquer the land, the struggles people faced and the wonder of nature.

He climbed the cliffs, crawled into the caves, dove from the swimming rock, collected clams from the bottom of the pond, gigged and skinned frogs for their legs. He trapped muskrats for fur, hunted raccoon in the dead of night, and with only a stick hunted rabbits in the dead of winter.

His young outdoor life and nature tested him.

He walked to a one room stone schoolhouse uphill both ways. A stern but warm-hearted teacher, Mrs. Henry was instrumental in shaping his character as she shepherded him from the fourth to the eighth grade, A Montessori before its time. It was a great way to grow up.

His experiences inter-twined with snippets of fantasy lend themselves to the adventures Taelo leads the reader through.

Ron has told many similar stories to impart life values and influence the thinking of his children and now grandchildren. He feels stories are a wonderful means for parents and their children to engage in meaningful discussions about behavior and fundamental values and principles.

If you enjoyed this, try:

The Taelo Series by Ron Mueller
    Taelo: The Early Years
    Taelo: The Golden Feather
    Taelo: Journey of Discovery
    Taelo: Dangerous Passage
    Taelo: Condor Clan Slingers

A Taelo Story:
    The Name of the Child
    White Swan and Quiet Pheasant
    Broken Spear
    Floating Cloud
    Quiet Rabbit
    Busy Bee
    Little Otter & Talking Wren
    Burley Bear & Meadow Flower

Science Fiction Books by Ron Mueller
    The Door Series:
        The Door
        Delivery
        Journey Beyond

    The Savitar Series:
        Journey's End
        Savitar
        Confluence

    Single Science Fiction Books:
        Current Past and Future
        Event Survivors

Fiction Books by Ron Mueller

The Problem Solver Series:
    The Beginning
    Drug Lords
    Border Crossers

The Alex Evercrest Series:
   The Riverfront
   The Girl on the Grill
   Missing
   Maggot

Imagination by Courtney Huynh and Chloe Parker

QR Links to

ATWP.US web site

Published by: Around the World Publishing LLC.

9 781682 232071